# AT THE WATERHOLE

## BETH SHOSHAN

### ILLUSTRATED BY
### PIERS HARPER

Albury Children's

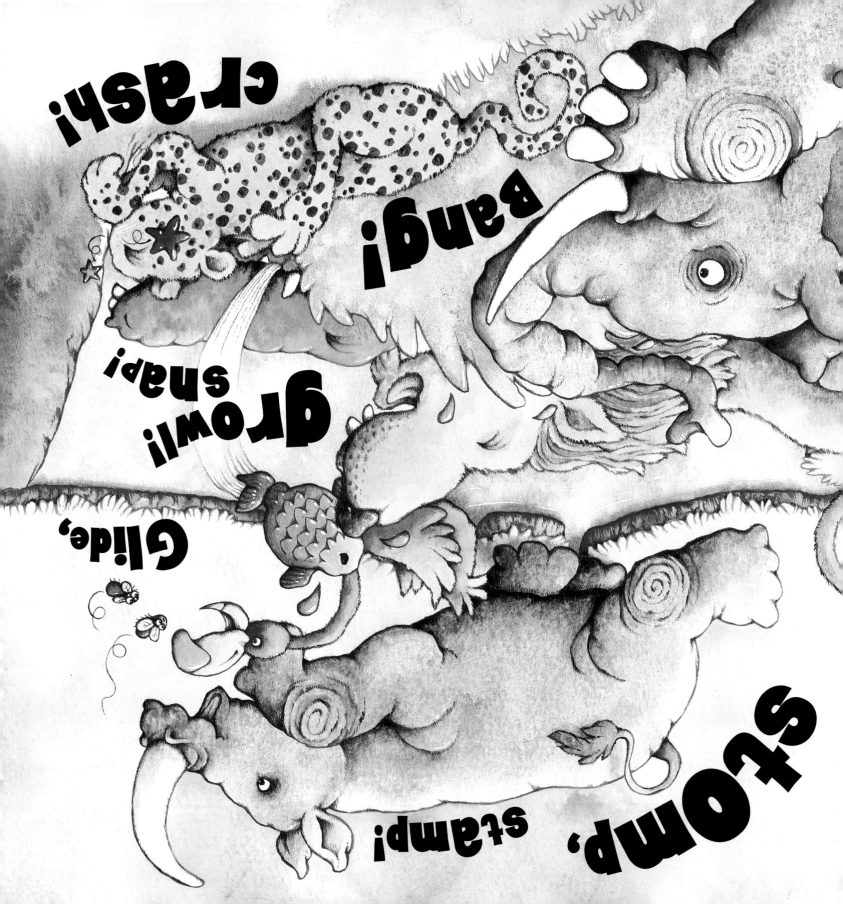

SlOOWW.

SLUGGISH,

sleepy,

rush!

race,

Wallop, wham,
thump, bump,
stomp, stamp.

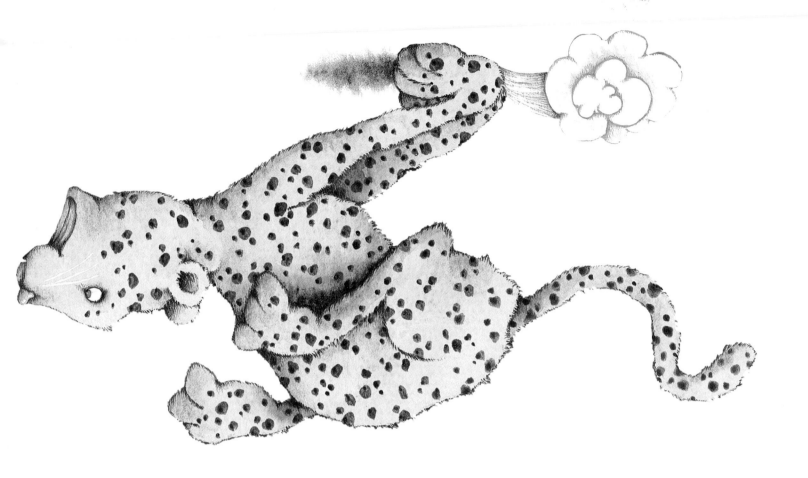

Published by Albury Books in 2017
Albury Court, Albury, Thame, OX9 2LP
United Kingdom

Text © Piers Harper • Illustrations © Piers Harper
The rights of Piers Harper to be identified as the
author and illustrator have been asserted by
them in accordance with the Copyright,
Designs and Patents Act, 1988

ISBN 978-1-909958-81-80 (paperback)

A CIP catalogue record for this
book is available from
the British Library
10 9 8 7 6 5 4 3
Printed in China

FOR (SM)ASHER
B.s.

FOR ALEX
P.H.